This book belongs to

ORCHARD BOOKS
338 Euston Road London NW1 3BH
Orchard Books Australia
Level 17/207 Kent Street, Sydney, NSW 2000

First published in 2014 by Orchard Books
ISBN 978 1 40833 133 0

HASBRO and its logo, MY LITTLE PONY and all related
characters are trademarks of Hasbro and are used with permission.

© 2014 Hasbro. All rights reserved.

A CIP catalogue record for this book is
available from the British Library.

3 5 7 9 10 8 6 4 2

Printed in China

Orchard Books is a division of Hachette Children's Books,
an Hachette UK company.
www.hachette.co.uk

Adult supervision is recommended for all
baking and cooking activities, and when
glue, paint, scissors and other
sharp points are in use.

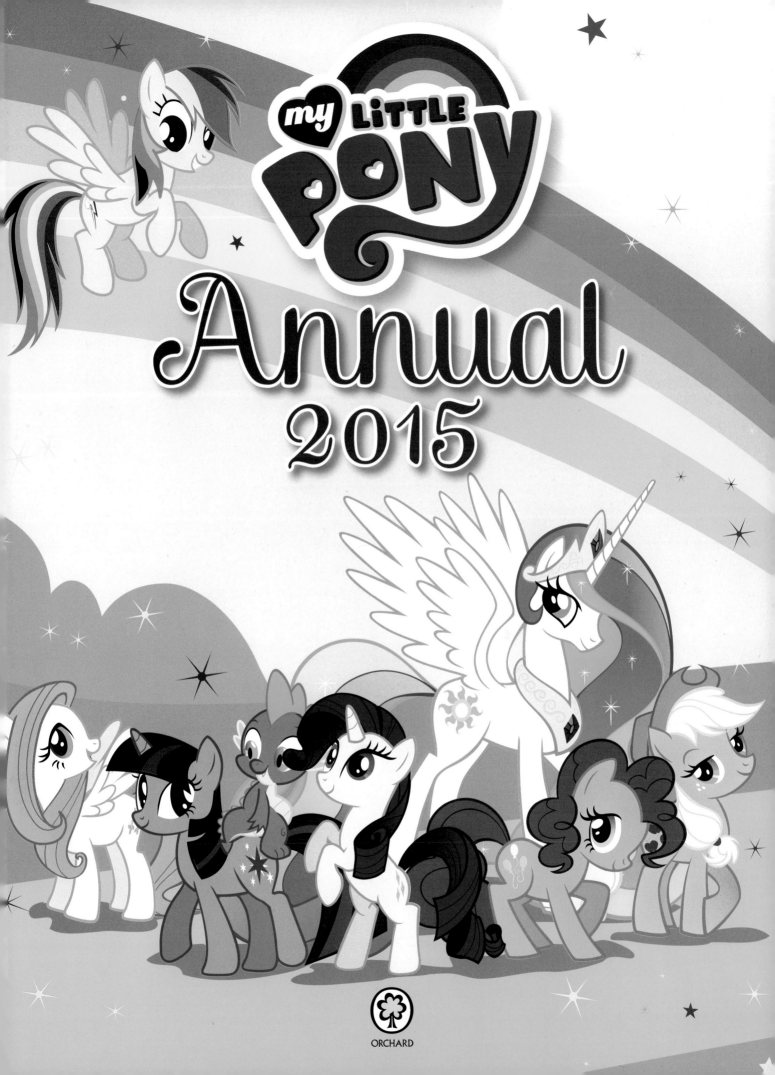

Contents

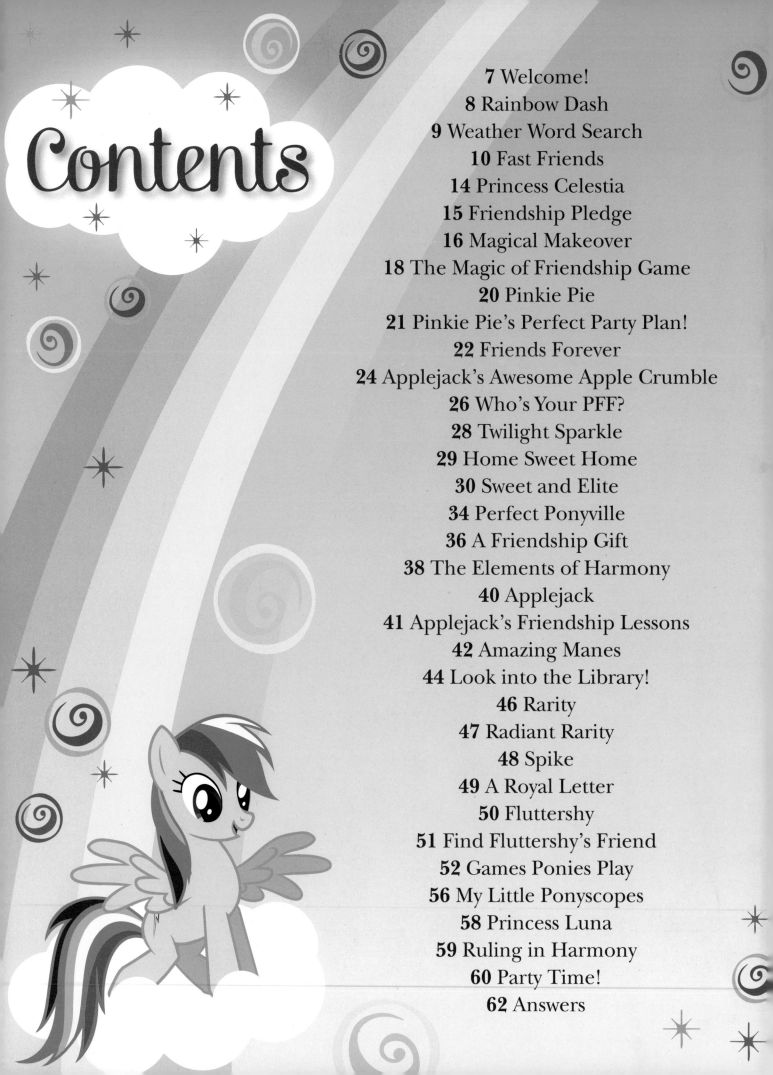

7 Welcome!

8 Rainbow Dash

9 Weather Word Search

10 Fast Friends

14 Princess Celestia

15 Friendship Pledge

16 Magical Makeover

18 The Magic of Friendship Game

20 Pinkie Pie

21 Pinkie Pie's Perfect Party Plan!

22 Friends Forever

24 Applejack's Awesome Apple Crumble

26 Who's Your PFF?

28 Twilight Sparkle

29 Home Sweet Home

30 Sweet and Elite

34 Perfect Ponyville

36 A Friendship Gift

38 The Elements of Harmony

40 Applejack

41 Applejack's Friendship Lessons

42 Amazing Manes

44 Look into the Library!

46 Rarity

47 Radiant Rarity

48 Spike

49 A Royal Letter

50 Fluttershy

51 Find Fluttershy's Friend

52 Games Ponies Play

56 My Little Ponyscopes

58 Princess Luna

59 Ruling in Harmony

60 Party Time!

62 Answers

WELCOME!

Dear friend,

We are so pleased you are here to join us. Books are one of my favourite things in the whole world and this one is super-special!

Inside we'll be showing you all around Equestria. We're going to have SO much fun together!

So what are you waiting for — turn the page and join us for friendship, magic and adventures!

Love,
Twilight Sparkle xxx

RAINBOW DASH

Rainbow Dash is the fastest pony in Equestria!

Home: Rainbow Dash lives in a cloud house, high above Ponyville.

Favourite activity: More than anything else, Rainbow Dash loves to fly . . . FAST!

Rainbow Dash's job: This little Pegasus has a very important job – she looks after the skies above Ponyville *and* makes sure the weather is just right!

Pony ambition: Rainbow Dash would love to join elite flying team The Wonderbolts.

Did you know . . . When she was younger, Rainbow Dash flew so fast she broke the air-speed record and was awarded a rainbow that shot out behind her like a jet stream!

Each pony friend represents a spirit of harmony. Rainbow Dash represents LOYALTY

Weather Word Search

Rainbow Dash speeds around the skies of Equestria, making sure the weather is just perfect! Can you find the six weather words hidden in this grid? Once you've found them all, decorate the page with stickers of the different types of weather.

**RAINBOW   THUNDER   MIST
CLOUDS   SNOW   SUNSHINE**

R	L	L	T	H	U	N	D	E	R
A	E	I	O	T	S	L	L	L	Y	N
I	K	N	P	W	X	M	I	S	T
N	H	R	Z	I	A	O	P	X	Y
B	G	O	Y	E	Y	W	L	U	G
O	C	L	O	U	D	S	K	R	F
W	J	W	Q	W	R	N	Y	S	D
M	D	S	L	A	E	O	H	T	S
U	E	S	I	H	D	W	R	H	W
S	U	N	S	H	I	N	E	K	L

FAST FRIENDS

It was a sunny day in Ponyville, and Applejack and Rainbow Dash were playing a game of horseshoes. Rainbow Dash was in the lead until Applejack made a perfect throw.

"Yee-ha! *That's* how we do it down on the farm!" cried Applejack.

"I hate losing," frowned Rainbow Dash. She turned to her friend. "Applejack, I challenge you to an Iron Pony competition. A series of athletic contests to decide who's the best!"

"You're on!" cried Applejack.

Before long, everything was ready for the big competition. Twilight Sparkle agreed to be the judge, assisted by her friend Spike the Dragon. As ponies poured in to watch the contest, Spike cried, "Let the games begin!"

First up was the Barrel Weave. Applejack managed to weave through the barrels in 22 seconds. But then Rainbow Dash whizzed round in just 18 seconds. She was the winner!

"Are you sure you're not a rodeo pony?" teased Applejack, pleased for her friend.

Next up was Buck the Ball. Applejack kicked the ball high up into the sky! The score was even.

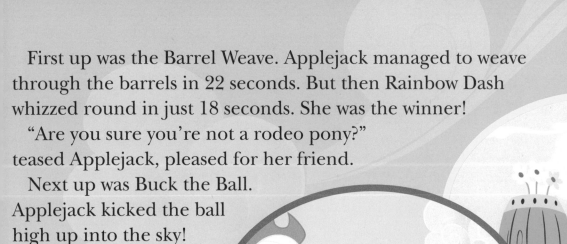

After lots more contests, including bronco bucking, lassoing and haybale tossing, Rainbow Dash was in the lead!

"All right, you two," called Twilight Sparkle. "This is the final event. Give it everything you've got!"

But Applejack had noticed that Rainbow Dash was using her wings in almost every event! When Rainbow Dash won the competition, Applejack was not happy.

"You're cheating!" she accused Rainbow Dash.

"You never said I couldn't use my wings!" Rainbow Dash answered back.

"Prove that you can win without your wings," said Applejack. "Tomorrow's the annual Running of the Leaves. I challenge you to race me in it."

"No wings, no problem!" scoffed Rainbow Dash.

The Running of the Leaves was a very important event. Without it, the autumn leaves of Equestria wouldn't fall from the trees.

"The race will begin in five minutes!" called Pinkie Pie. She and her co-announcer, Spike, were watching the action from a hot-air balloon in the sky.

As the competitors lined up, Applejack tied a rope around Rainbow Dash's wings to make sure she wouldn't use them. Twilight Sparkle trotted up to join them. "I'm racing too!" she announced.

"Well, see you at the finish line . . . tomorrow!" sniggered Rainbow Dash. Twilight Sparkle was more of a book pony than a racing pony!

The race began, with Pinkie Pie reporting on the action from her balloon. "Applejack is in the lead!" she called, jumping up and down with excitement.

But suddenly Applejack stumbled and fell into a heap. "Rainbow Dash tripped me!" she fumed.

"No, she didn't!" said Twilight Sparkle. "You just slipped."

Then, a few minutes later, Rainbow Dash fell over. "Applejack is cheating!" she grumbled.

"You should look where you're going," smiled Twilight Sparkle. "You tripped on that stump, see?"

But Rainbow Dash and Applejack wouldn't listen. Soon they were playing all kinds of tricks on one another as they each tried to get into the lead. As the finish line came into sight, Rainbow Dash's wings broke free and she flew up into the air. Applejack leapt after her and the two ponies span through the air, eventually rolling over the finish line . . . together!

"I won!" shouted Rainbow Dash.

"No, I won!" insisted Applejack.

"You tied . . . *in last place!*" Spike called down to them.

"I came fifth," said Twilight Sparkle, proudly showing them her medal. "I paced myself, just like my book said!"

Rainbow Dash and Applejack felt very ashamed. "Our behaviour was terrible," said Applejack.

"We weren't very good sports," agreed Rainbow Dash, hanging her head.

"It sounds to me like an important lesson has been learned," said a beautiful voice. It was Princess Celestia, ruler of Equestria! "I came to celebrate the Running of the Leaves," she explained. "But because you two were busy tricking each other instead of shaking down leaves, many of the trees are still covered."

Rainbow Dash and Applejack looked at each other. "I bet we can knock those leaves down, Princess," said Applejack. "Wanna go for a run, Rainbow Dash?"

"I'd love to!" Rainbow Dash agreed, and the two fastest ponies in Equestria galloped off together, the best of friends again!

Princess Celestia

Princess Celestia is the wise, kind and beautiful ruler of Equestria

Home: Princess Celestia rules the kingdom from her amazing castle in Canterlot.

Favourite colour: Yellow – the colour of the sun!

Favourite activity: The princess is very busy ruling the kingdom. Her most important job is helping the sun rise over Equestria each day *and* making sure that her subjects live in peace and harmony.

Family fact: Princess Luna is Princess Celestia's younger sister. They weren't friends for a very long time, but thanks to Twilight Sparkle and her pony pals, now they are loving sisters working side by side.

Did you know . . .
It is said that Princess Celestia is over 1000 years old!

Friendship Pledge

Princess Celestia knows that friendship is at the heart of a happy kingdom. To show you're a true friend of the ponies, put your hand on your heart and say these magical words. Sign your name at the bottom of the page!

I will love and care
for all of my friends,

From the start of each day
until the end.

We'll cherish each other
and laugh and care,

We'll have fun together
and play and share!

Signed

Freya Melville

Magical Makeover

Every pony deserves to look their best!
Can you make this little pony look as gorgeous
on the outside as she is on the inside?

The pony friends have some top tips for you,
and there are *lots* of stickers to help you make
a totally terrific transformation!

Always accessorise.
A scarf, hat or sunglasses
make all the difference
to a look.

Add a hat! I love wearing
my Stetson when I'm
working hard on the farm.
Yee-ha!

Close your eyes.
What does your dream
pony look like? Let your
heart guide you.

Wear pink, pink
and more pink!
It's the true colour
of fashion happiness.

Bright colours are
the best! Stand out from
the crowd using all the
colours of the rainbow.

Be inspired by nature!
Let your favourite wildlife
guide your choice of
colour and design.

THE MAGIC OF FRIENDSHIP GAME

1 START

2

3 You reach the Everfree Forest. It's very spooky! Hesitate and MISS A TURN

4

5

6 Applejack helps you make your way down a steep slope. MOVE FORWARD TWO PLACES

21

20

19 Rarity helps a sobbing sea serpent and he gives you a lift across the river. MOVE FORWARD TWO PLACES

18

22 You reach a ravine with no way across! MISS A TURN

23 Loyal Rainbow Dash mends the bridge across the ravine! Cross and MOVE AHEAD THREE PLACES

24

25 Night Mare Moon steals the Elements of Harmony GO BACK ONE PLACE

During their very first adventure together, the six pony friends had to travel to an ancient castle to find the missing Elements of Harmony and rescue Princess Celestia from the evil Night Mare Moon. Can you help the ponies make their way through the spooky forest to the castle?

Find your six pony friends on the sticker sheet. Choose one to play with, then stick this on to card to make a counter. You'll also need a dice and at least one friend to play with! Throw your dice and take it in turns to move around the board. The first one to reach the end is the winner. But be careful, Night Mare Moon's dark magic will try to stop you . . .

7

8

9

10
You run away from an angry lion!
MOVE BACK FIVE PLACES

11
Kind Fluttershy makes friends with the giant lion.
MOVE ON TWO PLACES

17
You reach raging river!
MISS A TURN

16

15

14
Clever Pinkie Pie shows you that laughter gives you courage!
TROT ON TWO PLACES

13

12

26

27
Twilight Sparkle realises she and her friends ARE the Elements of Harmony!
MOVE AHEAD TO 29

28

29

FINISH
30
You've done it!
Night Mare Moon's magic is destroyed and Princess Celestia is free!

Pinkie Pie

Pinkie Pie is full of energy, giggles and fun!

Home: Pinkie Pie lives above the Sugarcube Sweet Shoppe.

Favourite colour: Pinkie Pie just *loves* pink.
This cheery colour matches her upbeat personality!

Favourite activity: Pinkie Pie adores throwing parties
and entertaining her friends.

Best-loved food: This little pony has such a sweet tooth –
cakes and sweets are her favourite things to eat.

Most likely to say: "Are you loco in the coco?!"

Did you know . . . Pinkie Pie grew up on gloomy Rock Farm.
It was a *very* boring place for this fun-loving little pony.

Each pony friend represents
a spirit of harmony.
Pinkie Pie represents
LAUGHTER

PINKIE PIE'S PERFECT PARTY PLAN!

Here are Pinkie Pie's top tips for how to throw the perfect party. Remember that Pinkie Pie has a super-sweet tooth, so use your stickers to add extra cakes and treats to the page!

Ask a grown-up to help you bake vanilla cupcakes for the party and then ask your guests to decorate them! Make sure you have lots of icing and different decorations ready.

Have a theme and ask all your guests to dress up. Pinkie Pie loves to dress up as a princess!

Be creative with the decorating! Pinkie Pie loves to use streamers and balloons to customise a room.

Have lots of treats for your friends to eat. As well as yummy sweet treats, make cheese straws and mini pizzas for your guests to munch.

Music is very important. Before the party, create a playlist with lots of cheery music that your friends can dance to.

Games, games and more games! Pinkie Pie's favourite games include Pin the Tail on the Pony, Musical Chairs and Pass the Pony Parcel.

FRIENDS FOREVER

The super-perky owner of this alligator has to keep her pink hooves away from Gummy's mouth!

If you think tortoises are slow, think again! This pet can almost keep up with his super-speedy pony friend.

Fluttershy loves ALL animals,
but each and every pony has a
very special animal friend.
Can you work out from the clues which
animal is paired with which pony?
Draw a line between each
pair you spot.

Owls are very wise,
so this bird is well
matched to his
book-loving owner.

This pretty kitty has
an eye for fashion,
just like her owner!

This devoted dog
helps out down
at the farm
and is as
hard-working
as her owner!

23

Applejack's Awesome Apple Crumble

Giddy-up and get baking! This is one of Applejack's favourite recipes, straight from Sweet Apple Acres. You'll need a grown-up to help you make this.

Ingredients

3 Bramley cooking apples

100g granulated sugar

150g plain flour

75g of butter (softened)

① Pre-heat the oven to 180C/350F/gas mark 5.

② Peel, core and chop the apples into 1-2cm chunks.

Applejack's tip: If you use another kind of apple in your crumble, only use 75g sugar.

③ Place the chopped apples into a saucepan.

④ Add 2tbsp of water to the saucepan and 50g of sugar. Ask a grown-up to turn the hob to a medium heat and put the saucepan on the hob. Leave to stew until the apples become soft and mushy.

⑤ Place the mushy apples into an ovenproof dish.

⑥ Put the sieved flour and the remaining sugar into a mixing bowl. Add the butter and use your fingers to rub the mixture together until it looks like big breadcrumbs. Applejack loves to get her hooves messy here!

⑦ Sprinkle the mixture evenly on top of the stewed apple.

⑧ Ask a grown-up to put the crumble into the oven and cook for approximately 30 minutes.

⑨ Serve with vanilla ice-cream or custard. Dee-licious!

WHO'S YOUR PFF?

Take this quiz to find out who'll be your Pony Friend Forever!

What is your favourite colour?

Ⓐ Purple

Ⓑ All the colours of the rainbow – the brighter the better!

Ⓒ Pale yellow

Ⓓ Pink, pink and more pink!

Mostly Ⓐs – Your PFF is **Twilight Sparkle**. You're patient, studious and love books, just like Twilight Sparkle! You're a true friend with a heart of gold.

Mostly Ⓑs – Your PFF is **Rainbow Dash**. Super-speedy Rainbow Dash would be your perfect pony pal! You have lots of energy and always plan fun things to do.

What do you like to do at the weekend?

(A) Reading and relaxing

(B) Dashing around, trying to do as much as possible!

(C) Spending time with your animal friends

(D) Throwing an awesome PARTY!

What is your favourite animal?

(A) A wise owl

(B) Any animal that can fly fast and high in the sky!

(C) You love ALL animals but have a soft spot for fluffy bunny rabbits

(D) You'd love a perky pink poodle

What is your dream job?

(A) Teacher

(B) Racing driver... or pilot!

(C) Vet

(D) Party planner!

How would you describe yourself?

(A) Organised, studious and patient

(B) Energetic, loyal and FAST!

(C) Shy, caring and kind

(D) Playful, fun and girly!

Mostly (C)s – Your PFF is **Fluttershy**. With your kind heart and beautiful smile, you're the friend everyone turns to! Sometimes you feel a bit shy but you have lots of inner courage.

Mostly (D)s – Your PFF is **Pinkie Pie**. You're the life and soul of every party, with your sparkly eyes and super-positive outlook on life! You'd do anything to help your friends.

TWILIGHT SPARKLE

Twilight Sparkle is one of the kindest ponies you'll ever meet!

Home: Twilight Sparkle lives with Spike, her special dragon friend, in the Golden Oak Library in Ponyville. This means she can read books whenever she likes!

Favourite colour: Twilight Sparkle just loves purple – she finds it very peaceful and calming.

Favourite activity: This little pony adores reading and learning. She particularly likes to read all about magic.

Best friend: Twilight Sparkle loves all of her friends, but she thinks of her mentor, Princess Celestia, as a big sister.

Most likely to say: "We'll do everything by the book!"

Each pony friend represents a spirit of harmony. Twilight Sparkle represents **MAGIC**

HOME SWEET HOME

Twilight Sparkle and Spike live in the Golden Oak Library. But there are five objects in the library that really shouldn't be there! Can you spot them all? Draw a circle around each one.

SWEET AND ELITE

Rarity and her cat Opalescence were very excited to be visiting Canterlot. Twilight Sparkle had even arranged for them to stay in a beautiful suite at Princess Celestia's castle!

Rarity wondered how she could thank Twilight Sparkle for arranging such a special treat. As she saw a fabulously-dressed pony trot by, she had an idea. "I'll make an ensemble for Twilight Sparkle to wear to her birthday party this weekend! Perfect!"

Rarity got to work. She sketched the most amazing outfit *ever*, then went out and bought material to make her fabulous creation.

On her way back to the castle, Rarity bumped into Fancy Pants, a very well-known and important pony. Fancy Pants was *extremely* impressed to hear that Rarity was staying at Canterlot Castle with the princess. "You are obviously worth knowing!" exclaimed the posh pony.

"Listen," he continued, "I have a VIP box reserved at the Wonderbolts Derby this afternoon. Would you be so kind as to join me and a few of my companions there?"

Rarity knew that she didn't have time to make Twilight Sparkle's party dress *and* go to the derby. "But Fancy Pants is *the* most important pony in Canterlot," she said. "I just have to go!"

At the Wonderbolts Derby, Rarity headed up to the VIP box. The other Very Important Ponies wondered who she was and what she was doing there! Rarity was so keen to impress the posh ponies, she lied and told them that she knew the Wonderbolts' trainer!

"I told you all this was an important pony!" announced Fancy Pants to the crowd. Rarity gulped. She hadn't meant to tell a lie! But she soon forgot all about it as she was invited to all the society events in Canterlot – from a gallery opening to a charity auction!

"I'm becoming the most popular pony in Canterlot!" Rarity thought happily as she got ready for yet another event. "And I'm sure I'll still have time to make Twilight Sparkle's party outfit."

Soon the time came for Rarity to return to Ponyville. But just as she was gathering her luggage, one final invitation arrived. It was to the Castle Garden Party; *the* premier event in Canterlot! Rarity knew she didn't have time to go to Twilight Sparkle's birthday party *and* the garden party.

"The garden party is just too important to miss!" Rarity decided. She wrote to Twilight Sparkle, telling her she couldn't come back because her cat Opalescence was too ill to travel – which wasn't true at all!

But as Rarity opened the door to go to the garden party later that day, there were Twilight Sparkle, Pinkie Pie, Rainbow Dash, Applejack and Fluttershy shouting, "SURPRISE!"

"W…w…what are you all doing here?!" stammered Rarity.

"We're having my birthday party here," smiled Twilight Sparkle, "so you didn't have to miss it!"

Then Twilight Sparkle spotted the half-finished dress that Rarity had started to make for her. "I LOVE it!" she declared.

"You don't know how happy I am to hear you say that," Rarity said faintly.

Rarity and her friends went to the palace ballroom, where Twilight Sparkle's birthday party was being held.

"Look! There's another party in the castle grounds today," said Pinkie Pie. Rarity realised it was the garden party – she could see Fancy Pants and the other posh ponies chatting and laughing together!

Rarity sneaked back and forth between the two parties, and soon she was completely exhausted!

When her friends realised Rarity had been going to both parties, Rainbow Dash decided *all* the ponies should go to the fancy garden party. "Come on! Let's show 'em how to party Ponyville style!"

The garden party guests watched open-mouthed as Rarity's pony pals arrived. Pinkie Pie ate all the cake, Rainbow Dash ruined the croquet game and Applejack started digging up the garden, declaring, "this is a *garden* party, isn't it?!"

Then Twilight Sparkle told Fancy Pants that Rarity had designed her plain gown. "You mean . . . you know these ponies?" Fancy Pants asked Rarity.

After a pause, Rarity replied, "Yes, I do. They are my best friends and the most important ponies I know!" As the posh pony party guests gasped, Fancy Pants stepped forward. "Well, I think your friends are charming," he said kindly. "And I daresay every pony in Canterlot will be wanting one of these dresses!"

Later that day, Rarity told kind Princess Celestia what she had learned during her visit to Canterlot. "No matter where you go in life, you are the product of your home and your friends. And that is something always to be proud of, no matter what." And with that, Rarity set off back to her home and her best friends in Ponyville!

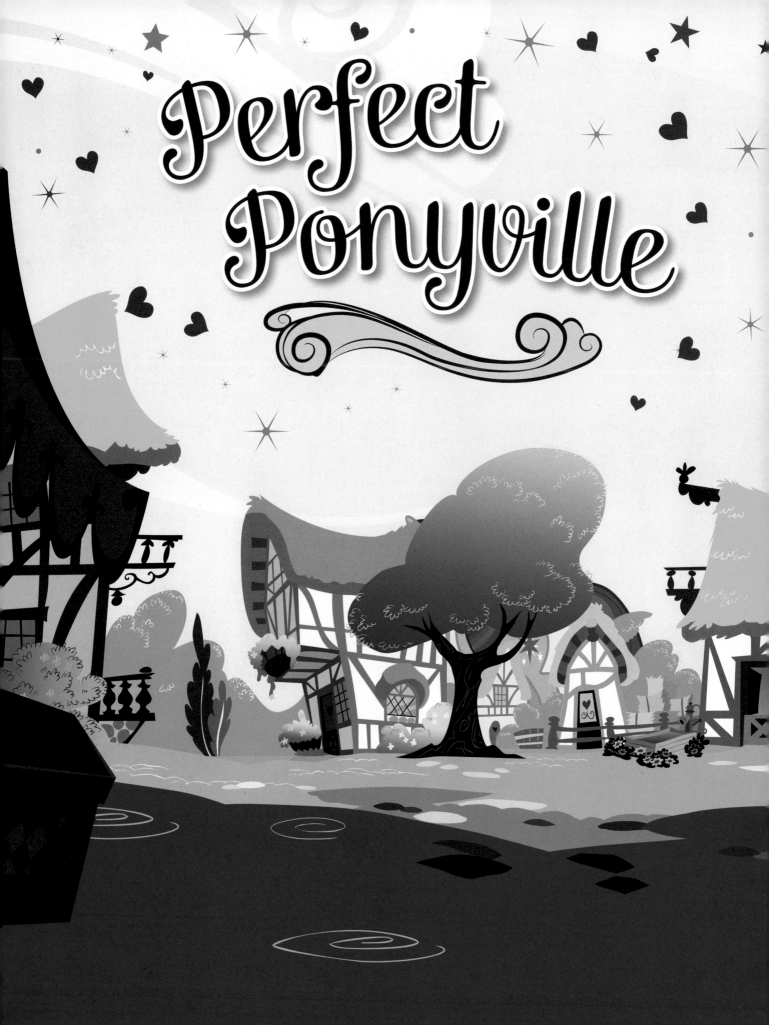

Perfect Ponyville

Ponyville is a small town full of hard-working, happy ponies! But where *are* all the ponies? Can you add them to the page using your stickers?

A FRIENDSHIP GIFT

The ponies love to show their friends just how much they care! Why not make a beautiful friendship bracelet as a special gift for your best friend?

You will need:

Embroidery thread or wool in two different colours

Sticky tape

A flat surface to tape the bracelet to (eg. a table or a clipboard)

To get started:

⭐ Ask a grown-up to cut two lengths of thread, each approximately 50cm long.

⭐ Tie a knot approximately 5cm from the top of the thread.

⭐ Tape the knot to your flat surface.

Starting position!

1 With the pink thread, make the shape of a '4'.

2 Bring the end of the pink thread under the yellow thread and through the hole. Pull the pink thread all the way through and then up towards the knot, holding the yellow thread in your other hand. Make sure you keep the pink thread on top.

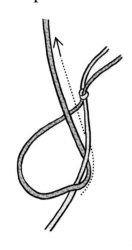

3 Next, make a backwards '4' using the yellow thread.

4 Pass the end of the yellow thread under the pink thread and through the hole.

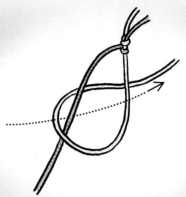

5 Pull the yellow thread all the way through and then up towards the knot, making sure that it stays on top.

6 Continue using this pattern (pink thread, yellow thread, pink thread, yellow thread) to your desired bracelet length. Then knot and tie around your wrist.

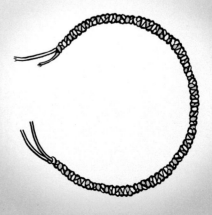

The Elements

The Elements of Harmony are six magical jewels that harness the power of friendship. Add a sticker of each pony and their Element to this page.

Twilight Sparkle embodies the spirit of **Magic**!

She needed the presence of five special friends to reveal her magic. The Element of Magic is a gold tiara studded with sapphires and a magenta star-shaped gem.

Pinkie Pie brings **Laughter** to the group!

The Element of Laughter is represented as a gold necklace with a blue balloon-shaped gem.

Rarity exudes **Generosity**!

The Element of Generosity is a gold necklace with a purple diamond-shaped gem.

# of Harmony

Rainbow Dash represents the Element of **Loyalty**.

The Element of Loyalty is represented as a gold necklace with a red thunderbolt-shaped gem.

Applejack represents **Honesty**.

The Element of Honesty is represented as a gold necklace with an apple-shaped gem.

Fluttershy embodies the spirit of **Kindness.**

The Element of Kindness is represented as a gold necklace with a butterfly-shaped gem.

APPLEJACK

Applejack is the sweetest, kindest farm gal in town!

Home: Applejack lives with her family at Sweet Apple Acres Farm, on the outskirts of Ponyville.

Favourite activity: Applejack is one hard-working pony! There are always plenty of jobs to be done on the farm, from picking apples to baking.

Applejack's family: Applejack has a huge family! Big McIntosh is her older brother, Apple Bloom is her little sister and then there's Granny Smith.

Applejack loves . . . to get her hooves muddy! She doesn't care if she is dirty or dusty or grubby, much to the surprise of Rarity.

Favourite accessory: Applejack believes in natural beauty, but she does love her Stetson hat and wears it almost every day!

Each pony friend represents a spirit of harmony. Applejack represents HONESTY

APPLEJACK'S FRIENDSHIP LESSONS

Well, hey there!
My friends and I have learned a LOT about friendship during our adventures.
Here are some of the most important things I've picked up.

Differences can be a good thing!

Rarity and I are very different. But we've learned that our differences mean that we each bring something very special to our friendship!

Accept help from your friends

When it was apple-picking season I was rushed off my hooves, but I thought I could do it all by myself! Eventually I realised how much easier and more fun it was with my friends by my side.

Friendship is more important than competition

When Rainbow Dash and I took part in the Running of the Leaves, we fought so much we both came last! Princess Celestia made us realise how silly we'd been.

Friends can make bad times great

When we all went to the Grand Galloping Gala we thought it would be the best night EVER! The gala turned out not to be fun, but we all enjoyed hanging out with each other.

Amazing Manes

It's amazing how much a new hairstyle can transform a look! Here are a few of Rarity's favourite styles.

The Magnificent Messy Ponytail

Applejack likes to keep things casual when she's hard at work on the farm. If you have longish hair, here's how to create the perfect relaxed ponytail.

1. Tip your head upside down and run your fingers through your hair to add volume.

2. If you have a fringe or layers at the front of your hair, separate a few pieces to frame your face.

3. Use your fingers to pull back most of your hair and secure in a high ponytail with a simple hairband. You don't want the band to be too tight as this look is all about keeping it casual!

The Perfect Plait

Sweetie Belle likes to make a couple of small plaits close to her forehead, leaving the rest au naturel! You can achieve this look even if you have short hair.

1. Take a small section at the front of your hair and plait it, then secure the end with a hairgrip.

2. Take another small section of hair from underneath the first and create a second plait, securing the end with a hairgrip.

3. Hide the ends of the plaits under your hair and keep the rest of your hair messy for a super-cool look!

Wow Waves!

Pinkie Pie loves to make her hair super wavy before she throws a party! This style works best on medium to long hair.

1. Spray your hair with water so it's a little damp.

2. Part the hair into four sections and twist each section around your finger tightly.

3. Repeat the twisting several times while the hair dries naturally.

4. Once your hair is dry, tip your head upside down and shake out the sections.

You Look Amazing!

Look Into the Library!

The magical Golden Oak Library is home to Twilight Sparkle and Spike the dragon. Study this scene for ten seconds and then cover it up with a piece of paper. Now see how many of the questions you can answer correctly! Award yourself a star sticker for each one you get right.

Twilight Sparkle's bed has three horseshoes above it. True or false?

How many books are there on the middle shelf?

Twilight Sparkle's cutie mark is a collection of stars. True or false?

The quilt on the bed is pink with a heart pattern. True or false?

The bedroom curtains are a beautiful golden colour. True or false?

What is right in front of the window? Clue: Twilight Sparkle can use this to see across Ponyville!

Spike has a yellow tummy. True or false?

Rarity

Rarity is creative, glamorous and very generous!

Home: Rarity lives above her shop, the Carousel Boutique, in Ponyville.

Favourite activity: Rarity loves everything about fashion and style! She designs and makes all the clothes for her boutique and often creates outfits for her pony pals.

Rarity loves . . . to perform makeovers! She often tries to transform her pony friends and always experiments with new styles and accessories.

Did you know . . . Rarity has a magical unicorn horn, just like Twilight Sparkle!

Most likely to say: "A unicorn's not a unicorn without grace and beauty."

Each pony friend represents a spirit of harmony. Rarity represents GENEROSITY

Radiant Rarity

Rarity is always keen to try out new styles and fashions. Can you decorate Rarity's mane and tail, giving her a fabulous new hairstyle?

Don't forget to add an amazing outfit and use lots of colour!

Your stickers will really help you bring this picture to life.

SPIKE

Spike the dragon is Twilight Sparkle's faithful friend and sidekick!

This friendly baby dragon just loves adventures! He was very pleased to move to Ponyville, where there are lots of new ponies to meet.

Spike has the ability to magically deliver scrolls to and from Princess Celestia using his green fire breath.

Spike loves all sparkly jewels. He is a dragon after all, and *all* dragons love treasure!

Did you know . . . Spike has a crush on Rarity – he thinks she is *amazing*!

A ROYAL LETTER

Can you help Spike with this letter from Twilight Sparkle to Princess Celestia? Find the right stickers on the sticker sheet to fill in the gaps. Then Spike will send the letter to Princess Celestia using his magical fire breath!

Dearest

Today Spike and I paid a visit to

on her farm. She was baking lots of delicious

We were joined by   and

made sure

that the   shone all day long!

We all look forward to seeing you soon.
With love from
your faithful student,

xxx

FLUTTERSHY

Gentle Fluttershy is shy, sweet and serene!

Home: Fluttershy lives in a cottage near the Everfree Forest.

Favourite activity: This little pony loves to make friends with all animals, from tiny woodland creatures to powerful beasts!

Personality: Fluttershy is shy when she first meets new friends. But she can be very brave when it comes to enjoying an adventure.

Best friend: Fluttershy loves all her pony friends, but she adores her cute little white rabbit, Angel Bunny.

Did you know . . . Fluttershy is a Pegasus (a flying pony) – just like Rainbow Dash! Unlike Rainbow Dash, she is a nervous flier and is scared of heights.

Each pony friend represents a spirit of harmony. Fluttershy represents **KINDNESS**

Find Fluttershy's Friend

Help Fluttershy through the maze to reach Angel Bunny.

Start

Finish

GAMES PONIES PLAY

It was a sunny morning in Ponyville. Twilight Sparkle and her pony friends had their saddlebags packed and were off to catch an important train.

They were on their way to the Crystal Empire to visit Princess Cadance. The Crystal Empire was hoping to host the next Equestria Games – a very important event in Equestria – and Twilight Sparkle and her friends were forming a welcoming committee for the Games Inspector. They were hoping to convince her that the empire was the perfect place to host the games!

When they arrived at the train station, the ponies were blown away by how super, super sparkly the Crystal Empire was looking. "They must have had every pony in the empire out sprucing this place up!" gasped Applejack.

At the Crystal Empire Spa, Princess Cadance was delighted to see Twilight Sparkle and the other ponies.

The princess showed the friends around – there were masseurs, hair stylists and an amazing crystal mud bath to welcome the Games Inspector to the empire. Of course, Pinkie Pie jumped straight in!

Just as Princess Cadance was preparing to have a crystal headdress woven into her mane – an important tradition in the Crystal Empire – a messenger arrived with two pieces of bad news.

The first was that Princess Cadance's mane stylist was ill, and nobody else knew how to create the crystal headdress! Kind Rarity offered to have a go, although the very long list of instructions did make her nervous!

Rarity gulped. "I'll give it everything I've got!" she declared. "Besides, the Games Inspector isn't expected for several hours."

Unfortunately, the second piece of bad news was that the Games Inspector, Mrs Harshwhinny, was due on the next train, arriving in fifteen minutes' time!

Twilight Sparkle took control. Leaving Princess Cadance in the safe hooves of Rarity, she headed off with the other members of the welcoming committee to meet Mrs Harshwhinny at the train station.

"Mrs Harshwhinny's letter said that she would be carrying a flowery suitcase," said Twilight Sparkle, as they watched the train pull in.

"Look, that must be her!" cried Rainbow Dash, pointing at a pony who was stepping onto the platform.

The friends quickly gathered around the pony with the flowery case. She seemed quite overwhelmed as they offered to carry her bag and give her a tour of the Crystal Empire!

But little did the ponies know that there was *another* pony with a flowery suitcase waiting at the other end of the platform, and she didn't look happy at all . . .

At the Crystal Castle, the ponies continued to impress the visitor. She was amazed by their welcome tour. "I have travelled far and wide," she declared, "but I have never, ever been welcomed like this before!"

Back at the Crystal Empire Spa, Rarity was struggling with Princess Cadance's complicated hairstyle. It didn't look quite right!

"You have to buy me some time!" screeched Rarity when Twilight Sparkle dropped in to see how things were going.

Meanwhile, the other visitor with the flowery suitcase had reached the spa, and she was not happy . . .

Twilight Sparkle and her friends were desperately trying to keep their visitor happy, still sure that *she* was the Games Inspector. But when they reached the Crystal Empire Stadium, their guest galloped away!

When the ponies finally caught up with her, they realised that she *wasn't* the Games Inspector. She was just a normal pony on holiday. They'd made a terrible mistake!

The ponies split up to try and find the *real* Mrs Harshwhinny. After searching the entire empire, they ended up in the Crystal Empire Spa. There was Mrs Harshwhinny, sitting with the pony that they had thought was the Games Inspector!

Just at that moment, Princess Cadance appeared with an amazing manestyle, ready to greet the real Mrs Harshwhinny.

Rainbow Dash stepped forward. "Princess, we gave our welcome to the wrong pony and left the right one waiting at the station. We've completely ruined everything."

"Actually, you've done quite the opposite," said Mrs Harshwhinny.

"Huh?" Rainbow Dash looked very confused.

"I've just been hearing how this pony came to visit the Crystal Empire with no advance warning and, not knowing a single pony here, was just treated to the warmest, funnest, most fabulous reception she ever had!" explained Mrs Harshwhinny. "Anywhere that can give such an amazing welcome is a worthy host for the Equestria Games!"

As Princess Cadance announced the Games Inspector's decision later that day, hundreds of happy ponies gathered to celebrate in the sparkly streets of the Crystal Empire.

Twilight Sparkle and her friends travelled back to Ponyville the next day. They couldn't wait to return to the Crystal Empire to watch the Equestria Games in action!

MY LITTLE PONYSCOPES

AQUARIUS
(21st January–19th February)

You are an honest and loyal friend who has lots of good ideas.

TAURUS
(21st April–21st May)

You're a great friend with a warm heart! You are very loyal and can be a bit stubborn.

PISCES
(20th February–20th March)

You are very creative and a kind, sensitive friend. You can also be a bit of a dreamer!

GEMINI
(22nd May–21st June)

You love to socialise and have lots of friends. You find it hard to make decisions and are often running late!

ARIES
(21st March–20th April)

You have lots of energy and courage. You work well in a team, although you can be a bit of a daredevil!

CANCER
(22nd June–23rd July)

You are very loving, caring and imaginative. You are often surrounded by a big group of friends.

LEO
(24th July–23rd August)
You are the leader of the pack! You're super organised and can sometimes be a little bit bossy… but your friends always forgive you!

SCORPIO
(24th October–22nd November)
You bring giggles and excitement to every occasion! Plus, you're great at keeping secrets.

VIRGO
(24th August–23rd September)
Your friends really value your opinion as you're a very thoughtful and balanced person. You also like things to be just perfect!

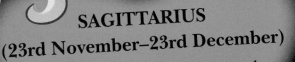

SAGITTARIUS
(23rd November–23rd December)
You are creative, sociable and lots of fun to be around. You love to make your friends laugh!

LIBRA
(24th September–23rd October)
You're generous and sociable and love to hang out in a big group. You always make time for your pals.

CAPRICORN
(23rd December–20th January)
You can be competitive and all your friends want to be in your team when you play a game! You're well known for your sense of humour and kind eyes.

Princess Luna

Princess Luna is Princess Celestia's little sister!

Princess Luna and Princess Celestia used to rule Equestria together, with Celestia looking after the day and Luna looking after the night. But Princess Luna became very angry that the ponies slept through each night and this anger turned her into Night Mare Moon, a wicked mare of darkness! Celestia banished her to the moon and it was only with the help of Twilight Sparkle and her pony friends that Night Mare Moon was transformed back into kind Princess Luna.

Best friend: Princess Luna is pleased to be friends with all the ponies again, but she adores her big sister Princess Celestia.

Did you know . . .
Night Mare Moon was banished to the moon for one thousand years!

Ruling In Harmony

Look at this beautiful old picture of Princess Celestia and Princess Luna. Can you copy this picture into the space below and colour it in using your pens and pencils?

PARTY TiME!

Princess Celestia is throwing an amazing party! Add lots of guests, party food and decorations to these pages to make it the best party Equestria has EVER seen!

ANSWERS

Weather Word Search

R	L	L	T	H	U	N	D	E	R
A	E	I	O	T	S	L	L	Y	N
I	K	N	P	W	X	M	I	S	T
N	H	R	Z	I	A	O	P	X	Y
B	G	O	Y	E	Y	W	L	U	G
O	C	L	O	U	D	S	K	R	F
W	J	W	Q	W	R	N	Y	S	D
M	D	S	L	A	E	O	H	T	S
U	E	S	I	H	D	W	R	H	W
S	U	N	S	H	I	N	E	K	L

FRIENDS FOREVER

The Elements of Harmony

Look Into The Library!

Twilight Sparkle's bed has three horseshoes above it. True or false?
A: False – there are two horseshoes

How many books are there on the middle she
A: Two

Twilight Sparkle's cutie mark is a collection of stars. True or false?
A: True!

The quilt on the bed is pink with a heart pattern. True or false?
A: False, it is blue with a stars and moon patte

The bedroom curtains are a beautiful golden colour. True or false?
A: True

What is right in front of the window?
Clue: Twilight Sparkle can use this to see across Ponyville!
A: A telescope

Spike has a yellow tummy. True or false?
A: False, Spike's tummy is green!

HOME SWEET HOME

A ROYAL LETTER

Dearest

Today Spike and I paid a visit to

on her farm she was baking
lots of delicious

We were
joined by   and

                          made sure

that the   shone all day long!

We all look forward to seeing you soon.
With love from
your faithful student.

xxx

Find Fluttershy's Friend

Start

Finish

EXPLORE THE MAGICAL WORLD OF MY LITTLE PONY!

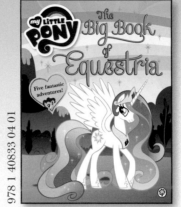

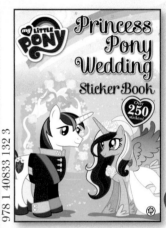